If MUM and Me were MerMaids

Hodder Children's Books

A division of Hachette Children's Books

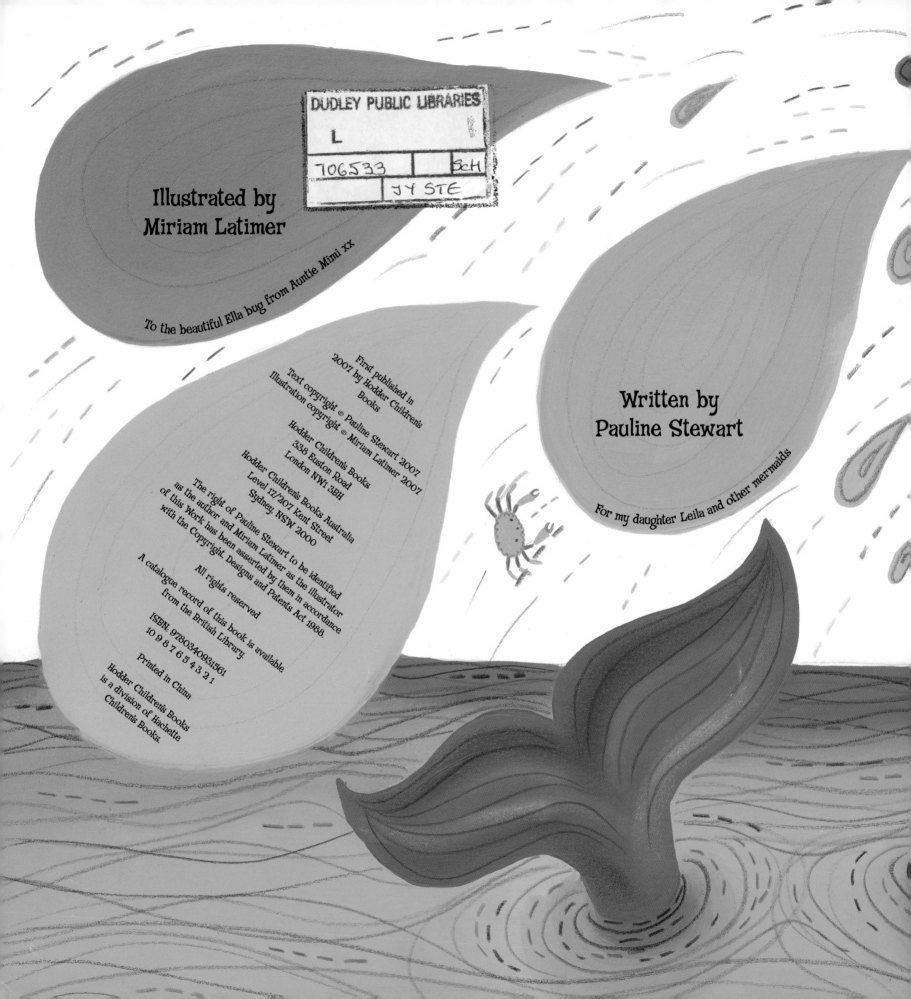

Illustrated by
Miriam Latimer

To the beautiful Ella bug from Auntie Mimi xx

Written by
Pauline Stewart

For my daughter Leila and other mermaids

First published in
2007 by Hodder Children's
Books

Text copyright © Pauline Stewart 2007
Illustration copyright © Miriam Latimer 2007

Hodder Children's Books
338 Euston Road
London NW1 3BH

Hodder Children's Books Australia
Level 17/207 Kent Street
Sydney, NSW 2000

The right of Pauline Stewart to be identified
as the author and Miriam Latimer as the illustrator
of this Work has been asserted by them in accordance
with the Copyright, Designs and Patents Act 1988.

A catalogue record of this book is available
from the British Library.

ISBN: 9780340931561
10 9 8 7 6 5 4 3 2 1

Printed in China

Hodder Children's Books
is a division of Hachette
Children's Books.

If MUM and Me were MerMaids,

We'd play every day, And sit upon the shiny rocks And braid our hair this way.

If Mum and Me were Mermaids,

We'd dive into the sea,

Mermaids can swim anywhere,

We'd be quite safe, you see.

If Mum and Me were Mermaids,

We'd swim from bay to bay,

Play hide-and-seek with visitors,

Then quickly

Swim away.

If Mum and Me were Mermaids,

We'd clean the coral reef,
Untangle all the seaweed,
Help dolphins brush their teeth.

If Mum and Me were Mermaids,

We'd search for shells and things,
Look for gold and diamonds,
And turn them into rings.

If Mum and Me were Mermaids,

We'd picnic on the beach,

We'd sip our cocoa milkshakes,

And eat the juiciest peach.

If MUM and Me were MerMaids,

We'd go dancing in the tide,
And do the 'Hula Ripple,'

While we shake from side to side.

If MUM and Me were Mermaids,

If Mum and Me were Mermaids,

We'd sparkle every day,

We'd laze upon the shiny rocks...

And never leave...

We'd
stay!